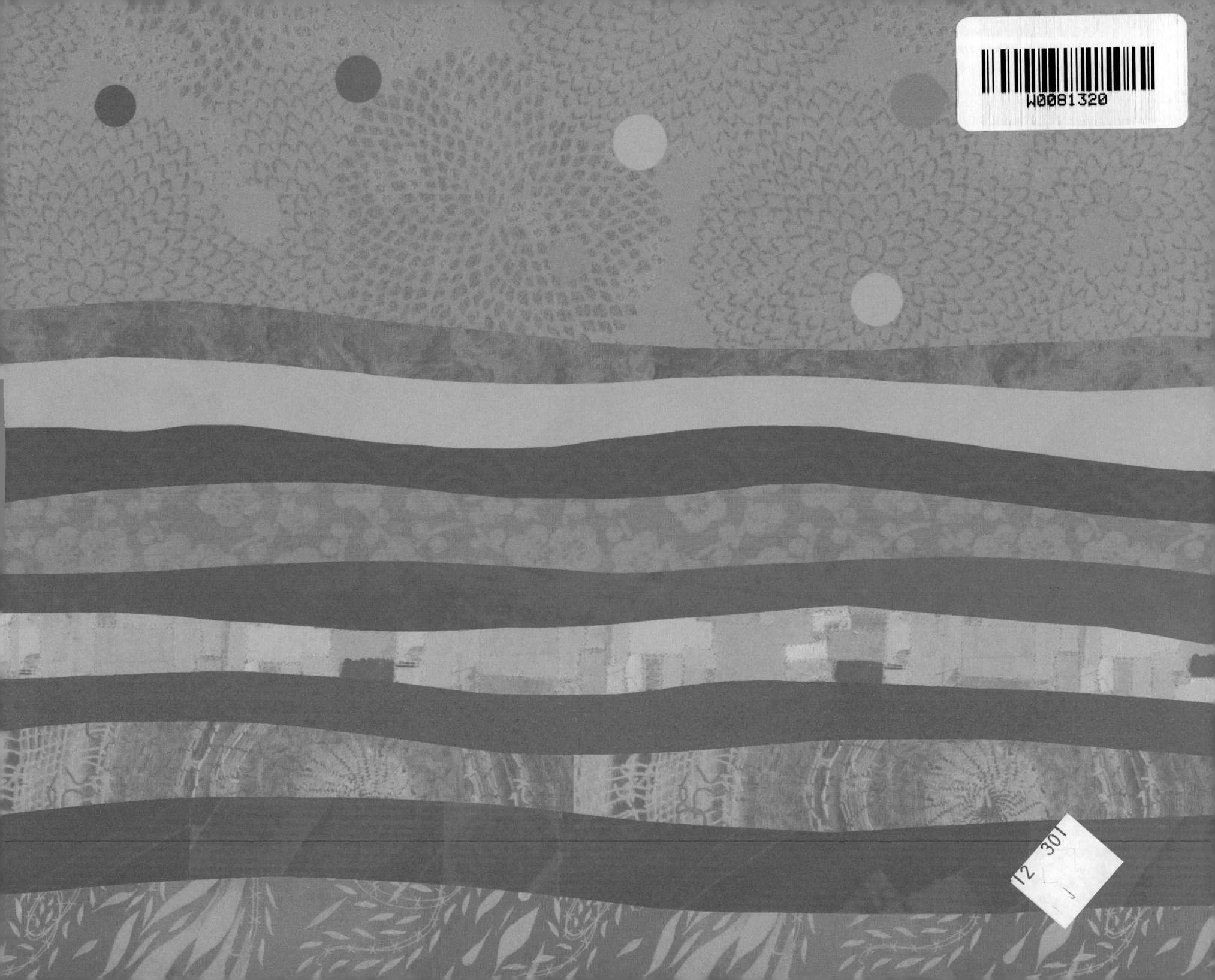

Some of Us

A Story of Citizenship and the United States

By Rajani LaRocca

Illustrated by Huy Voun Lee

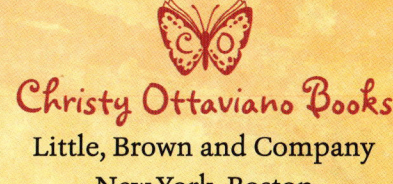

Christy Ottaviano Books
Little, Brown and Company
New York Boston

Some of us are born American.

Some choose.

We may come from
across the world,

or quite nearby.

Some of us are babies,
carried in hopeful arms;

some are six, or sixteen, or sixty.

We leave the countries of our birth and come here
by boat, and plane,

and car,

and train,

and foot.

We leave loved ones,

important jobs, beloved places;
we leave behind all we know.

FLOSSIE WONG-STAAL

I. M. PEI

Some of us are invited to study or work because of particular talents or training.

JESÚS FERREIRA

RIHANNA

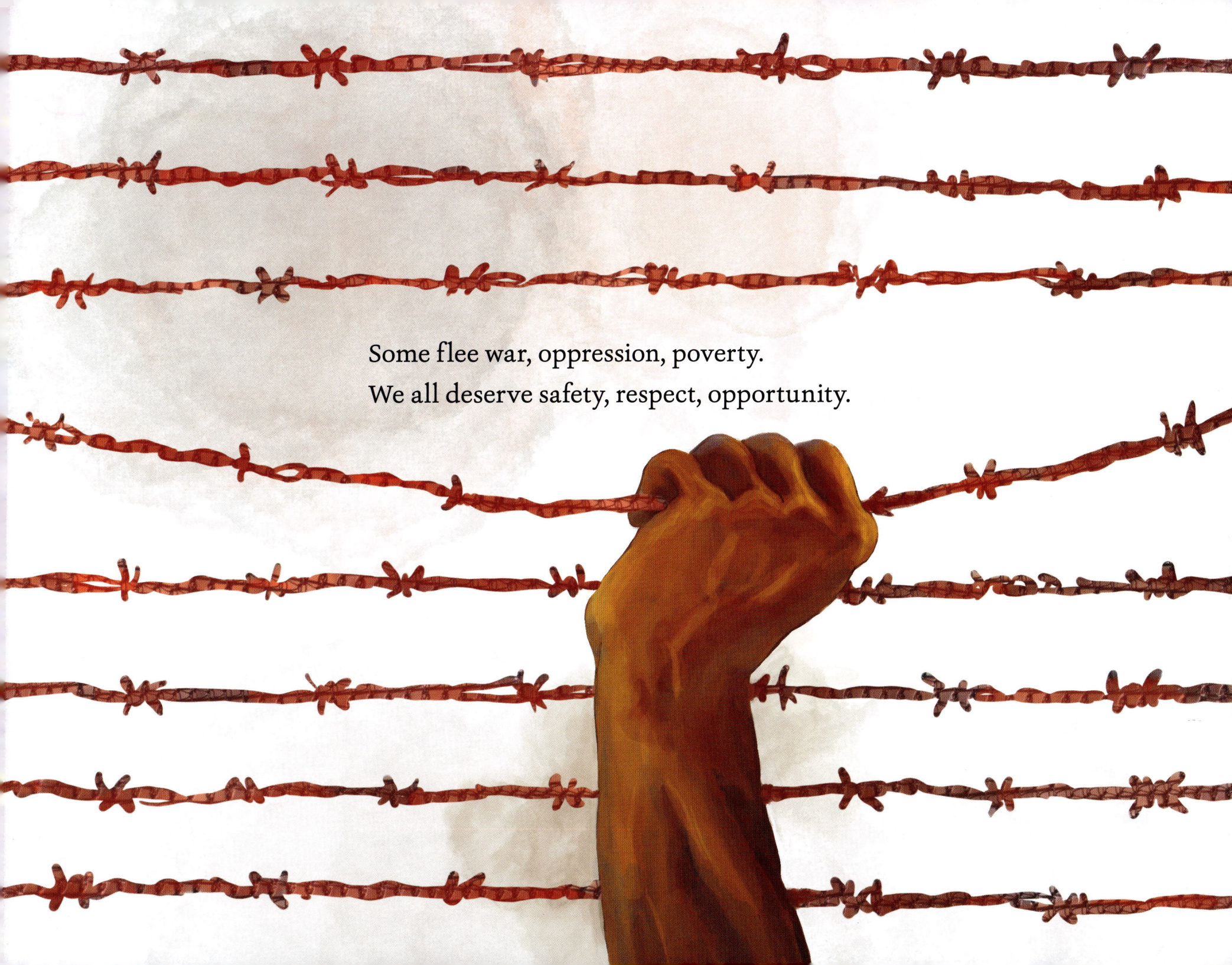

Some flee war, oppression, poverty.
We all deserve safety, respect, opportunity.

We bring with us our languages,
our cuisines,
our customs, clothing,
music, stories, histories.
We bring hard work and determination,
intelligence and skill,
optimism,
joy.

We learn and teach,
work and rest,
live freely
as we contribute
to our new communities.

We bring threads from the countries of our birth
and add to the rich tapestry of our new home,
a place we grow to love.

And after years,
without relinquishing who we are
or where we came from,
if we choose,
if we are fortunate,
we can become
naturalized citizens.
We can become
American.

We study how US democracy works.

We take a test and do an interview to demonstrate our understanding.

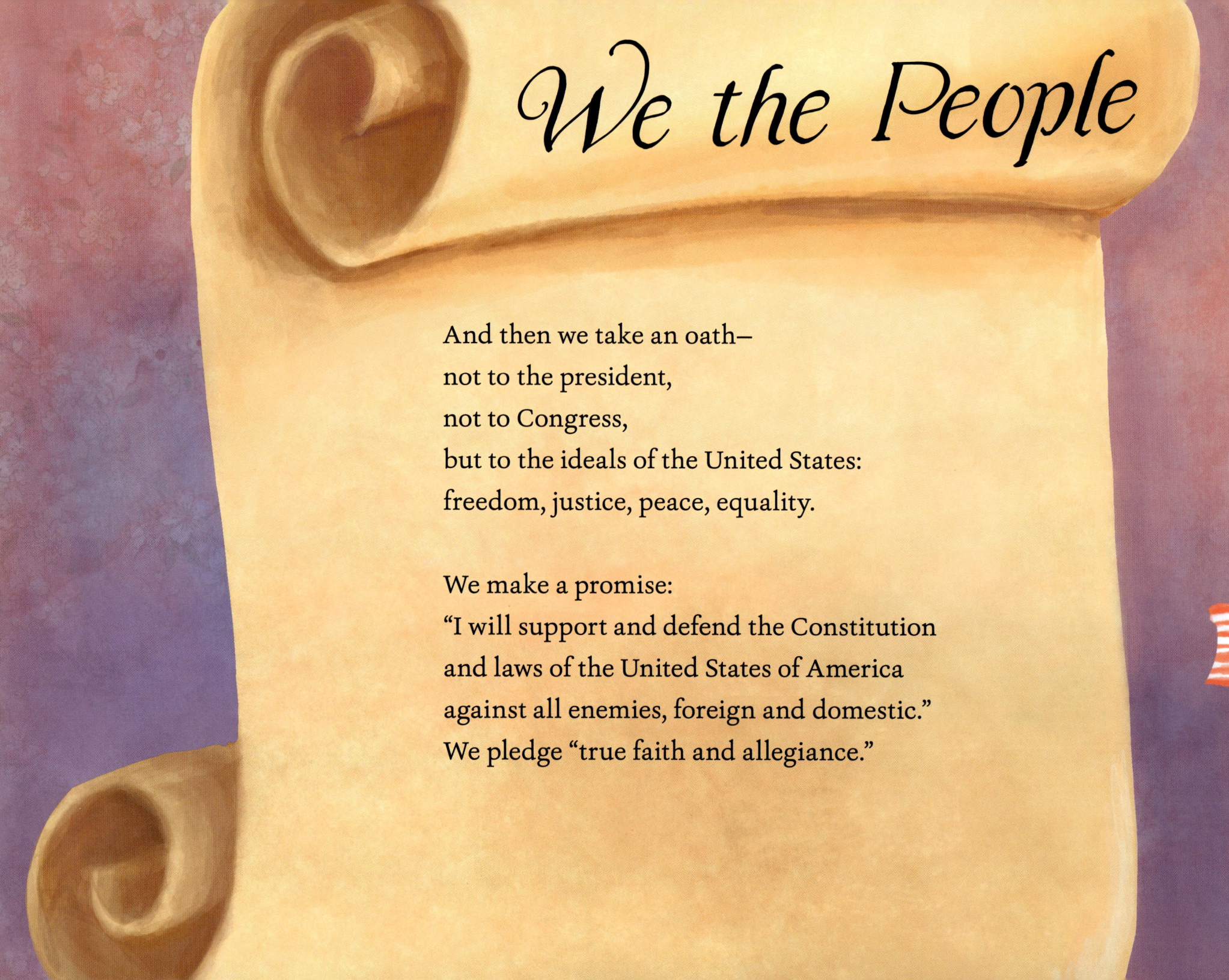

We the People

And then we take an oath—
not to the president,
not to Congress,
but to the ideals of the United States:
freedom, justice, peace, equality.

We make a promise:
"I will support and defend the Constitution
and laws of the United States of America
against all enemies, foreign and domestic."
We pledge "true faith and allegiance."

In return for accepting these responsibilities, we receive rights:

to speak our beliefs;
to worship, or not;
to be treated fairly under the law.

We can sign up to vote,
or run for elected office.
We can fully participate
in the governing of
the country we love.

Some of us are born to it.

Some of us choose.

And we are all American.

★ AUTHOR'S NOTE ★

Citizenship is the legal relationship between a country and a person in which the person receives certain rights and freedoms in exchange for promising loyalty to and respect for the ideals and laws of the country. People born in the United States, or whose parents are US citizens, are given US citizenship automatically. Under certain circumstances, people who move to the United States can choose to become naturalized citizens.

I was born in India and immigrated to the United States with my parents as a baby. When I was fifteen, I became a naturalized citizen. My father had acquired his citizenship years earlier and could have given it to me at the same time, but my parents wanted me to make this choice for myself.

Since I had been raised and educated in the United States, I had already learned a lot about how our democracy works, but I still studied for the test and interview. The day I went to the courthouse and took the naturalization oath with a group of wonderful fellow immigrants was surprisingly emotional. I will never forget raising my right hand and promising to defend the United States and its Constitution, to give my allegiance to this country. That was when I gained the rights, privileges, and responsibilities of being a citizen of the United States. That night, although I'd lived in the United States for almost my entire life, we celebrated with friends, also immigrants, who moved me to tears when they presented me with a "Welcome to the USA" cake. Since then, I have joyfully voted in every election that I could.

The United States of America has never been a country of just one type of people. Indigenous peoples have been here since long before the first European settlers arrived. Enslaved people were brought here against their will. And immigrants have chosen to come here from all over the world.

Since this country was founded, immigrants have made our lives stronger and better. Choosing to immigrate and eventually take the oath of citizenship can help people recognize how precious our freedoms are, and how we cannot take them for granted.

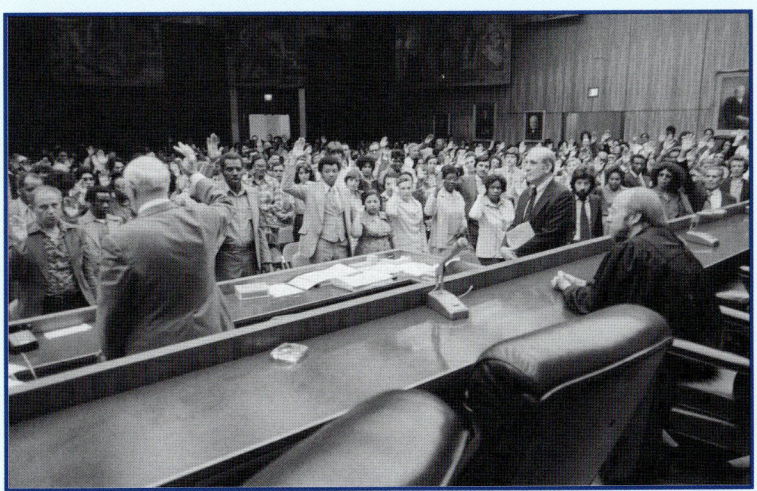

New US citizens taking the oath of allegiance during a naturalization ceremony in Brooklyn, New York, 1979.

But the history of US immigration and citizenship is somber. Time and again, people have been unfairly denied the right to immigrate due to arbitrary or racist laws. And for hundreds of years, the rights of citizenship have belonged only to a few, excluding many people who have lived in, worked in, and helped build our country from the beginning.

The Naturalization Act of 1790 allowed only free white immigrants to apply for citizenship after living in the country for at least two years. In 1868, the Fourteenth Amendment granted citizenship to people born in the United States, irrespective of race, but the law excluded Indigenous Americans who lived on reservations. In 1870, the Fifteenth Amendment gave Black men the right to vote—but in many places, that right was denied by state and local governments until the Voting Rights Act of 1965 outlawed their discriminatory practices.

Although women were considered citizens, they did not have the right to vote until the Nineteenth Amendment was ratified in 1920.

It wasn't until the Indian Citizenship Act in 1924 that all Indigenous Americans—the very first inhabitants of this land—were considered US citizens.

And it wasn't until the Immigration and Nationality Act of 1952 that Asian immigrants were allowed to become naturalized citizens.

Today, there are many people who were brought to this country as children, but as "undocumented" residents. They do not have the opportunity to become citizens, even though they came and were raised here without making the choice themselves.

Immigration and citizenship continue to be divisive issues that we struggle with as a country. That said, born or naturalized, all US citizens have the same rights and responsibilities. And we must all choose to engage in our democracy to protect everyone's rights and freedoms.

★ BEYOND CITIZENSHIP: THE RIGHTS OF ALL PEOPLES ★

While this book focuses on the rights and responsibilites of US citizenship and the many paths toward it, all people—regardless of immigration status, country of residence, or country of birth—hold unimpeachable human rights, which have been outlined in the United Nations' Universal Declaration of Human Rights, a document created in 1948. They are summarized below.

All of us are born free and equal
and should treat one another with dignity and respect,
regardless of race, gender, country, religion, language,
political opinion, or social status.

All of us have the right to live as we wish,
to be free from cruelty and enslavement,
to have a country to which we belong,
to move freely within and across countries,
and to escape persecution.

All of us have the right to be protected by laws,
to have those laws applied to us equally,
and to seek justice when our rights have been violated.

All of us, when we are old enough,
have the right to choose whether and whom to marry
and to create families.

All of us have the right to work, to be paid fairly for that work,
and to have rest and holidays.

All of us have the right to live healthy lives,
with food, shelter, safety, and education.

All of us have the right to hold opinions
and express them freely, to gather peacefully in groups,
and to participate in and enjoy the arts.

We, the people,
are the basis for government.

All of us have the right to participate in governing
and to freely elect our leaders.

No person or country should limit these rights and freedoms
except to ensure them for all.

★ SELECTED BIBLIOGRAPHY ★

For more information about United States civics, individual rights, and immigration history, you can visit the following online resources:

National Archives. "Voting Rights Act (1965)." Milestone Documents. https://www.archives.gov/milestone-documents/voting-rights-act.

National Museum of American History. "Defining Citizenship." *American Democracy: A Great Leap of Faith*. https://americanhistory.si.edu/explore /exhibitions/american-democracy.

United Nations. "Universal Declaration of Human Rights." About Us. https://www.un.org/en/about-us/universal-declaration-of-human-rights.

U.S. Citizenship and Immigration Services. "Should I Consider U.S. Citizenship?" Citizenship Resource Center. https://www.uscis.gov/citizenship /learn-about-citizenship/should-i-consider-us-citizenship.

U.S. Department of State. "The Immigration and Nationality Act of 1952 (The McCarran-Walter Act)." Office of the Historian. https://history.state.gov /milestones/1945-1952/immigration-act.

For all of us. —RL

For all Americans and soon-to-be Americans:
Bring your dream and your hope, your culture and your hard work.
Together let's share in making this country beautiful. —HVL

About This Book

The illustrations for this book were done in Procreate. The artist also used cut paper samples throughout. This book was edited by Jessica Anderson and designed by Angelie Yap with art direction from Tracy Shaw. The production was supervised by Lillian Sun, and the production editor was Jake Regier. The text was set in Ashbury, and the display type is Balford.

Text copyright © 2025 by Rajani LaRocca • Illustrations copyright © 2025 by Huy Voun Lee • Photograph on page 29 by Thomas J. O'Halloran. Courtesy of the Library of Congress, U.S. News & World Report Magazine Photograph Collection • Passport stamps © Victor Metelskiy/Shutterstock.com • Cover illustration copyright © 2025 by Huy Voun Lee • Cover design by Angelie Yap • Cover copyright © 2025 by Hachette Book Group, Inc. • Hachette Book Group supports the right to free expression and the value of copyright. The purpose of copyright is to encourage writers and artists to produce the creative works that enrich our culture. • The scanning, uploading, and distribution of this book without permission is a theft of the author's intellectual property. If you would like permission to use material from the book (other than for review purposes), please contact permissions@hbgusa.com. Thank you for your support of the author's rights. • Christy Ottaviano Books • Hachette Book Group • 1290 Avenue of the Americas, New York, NY 10104 • Visit us at LBYR.com • First Edition: May 2025 • Christy Ottaviano Books is an imprint of Little, Brown and Company. The Christy Ottaviano Books name and logo are registered trademarks of Hachette Book Group, Inc. • The publisher is not responsible for websites (or their content) that are not owned by the publisher. • Little, Brown and Company books may be purchased in bulk for business, educational, or promotional use. For information, please contact your local bookseller or the Hachette Book Group Special Markets Department at special .markets@hbgusa.com. • Library of Congress Cataloging-in-Publication Data • Names: LaRocca, Rajani, author. | Lee, Huy Voun, illustrator. • Title: Some of us : a story of citizenship and the United States / by Rajani LaRocca ; illustrated by Huy Voun Lee. • Description: First edition. | New York : Little, Brown and Company, 2025. | Includes bibliographical references. | Audience: Ages 5–10 | Summary: "Equal parts emotional and informative, here is a worthy picture book about citizenship and naturalization. This thoughtfully crafted text precisely breaks down the process by which new residents apply for and acquire US citizenship." —Provided by publisher. • Identifiers: LCCN 2023028877 | ISBN 9780316571753 (hardcover) • Subjects: LCSH: Naturalization—United States—Juvenile literature. | Citizenship—United States—Juvenile literature. | United States—Emigration and immigration—Juvenile literature. • Classification: LCC JK1759 .L | DDC 323.6/230973—dc23/eng/20240617 • LC record available at https://lccn.loc.gov/2023028877 • ISBN 978-0-316-57175-3 • PRINTED IN DONGGUAN, CHINA • APS ,07/25 • 10 9 8 7 6 5 4